PANDORA

Victoria Turnbull

CLARION BOOKS
Houghton Mifflin Harcourt
Boston   New York

Pandora lived alone,

in a land of broken things.

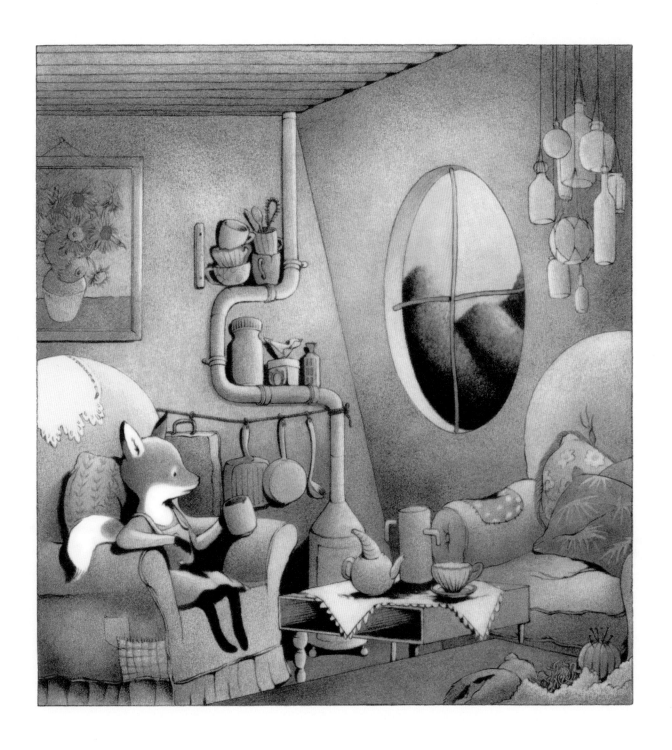

She made herself a handsome home
from all that people had left behind.
But no one ever came to visit.

So she spent her time gathering and repairing what she could,
bringing lost and forgotten things back to life.

Then one day . . .

something fell from the sky.

It was broken too,
but Pandora didn't know how to fix it.

So she made it as snug
as she could and watched over it
through the night.

Pandora's guest was
a little weak at first.

But as the days went by,
he grew stronger.

Soon he could hop about,
and then fly short distances.

But with gifts from faraway lands,

he always came back.

Until the day he didn't.

Once again, Pandora was alone.

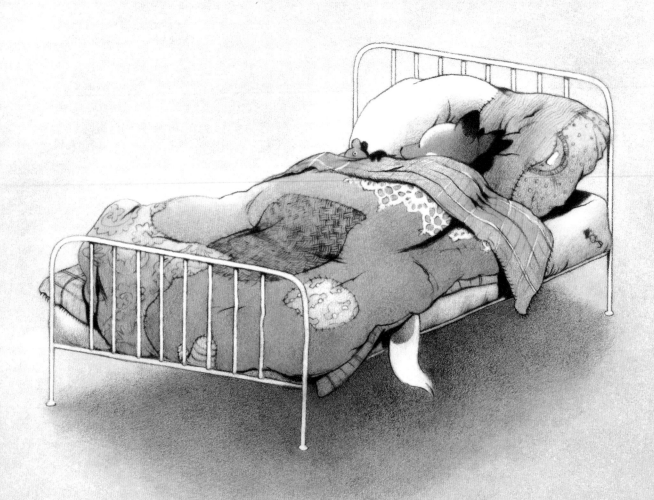

She thought her heart would break.

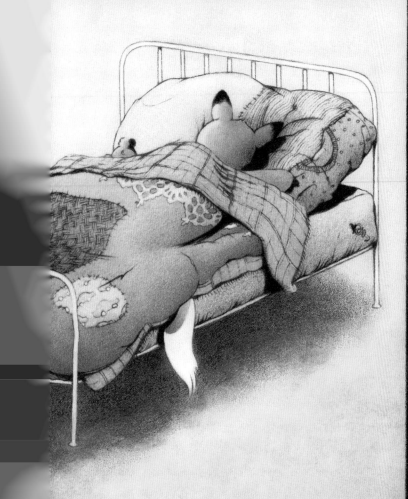

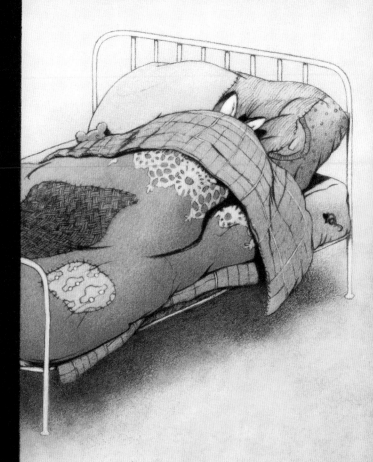

But day by day,

the world appeared

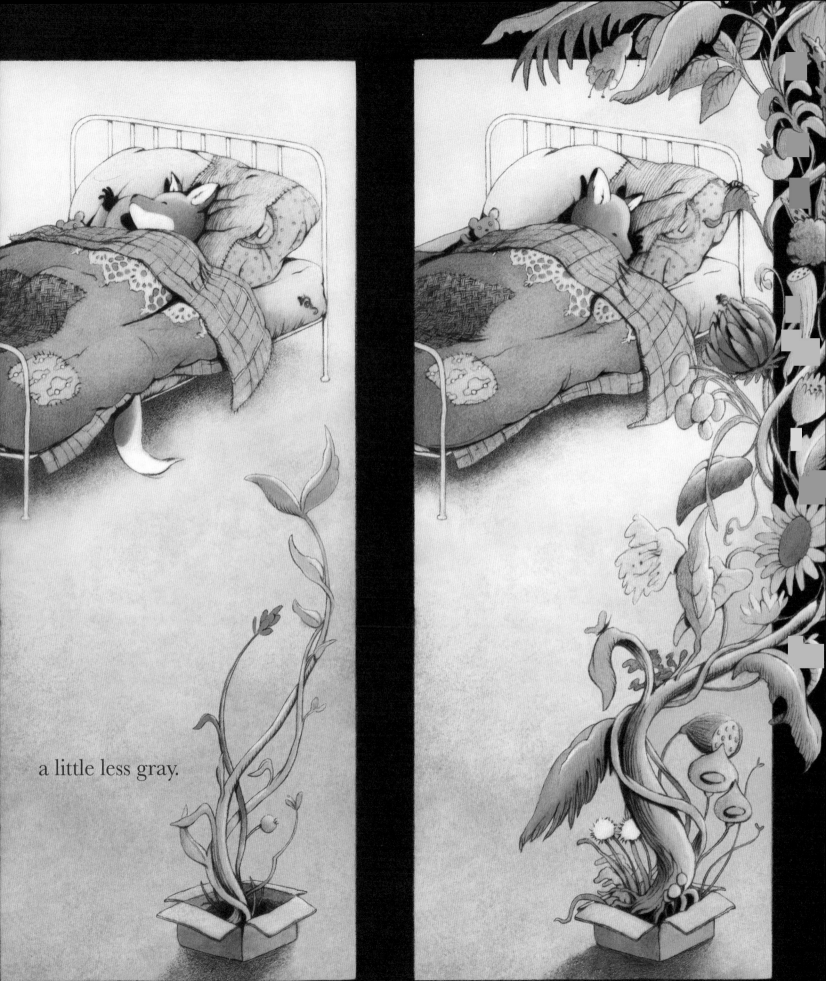

a little less gray.

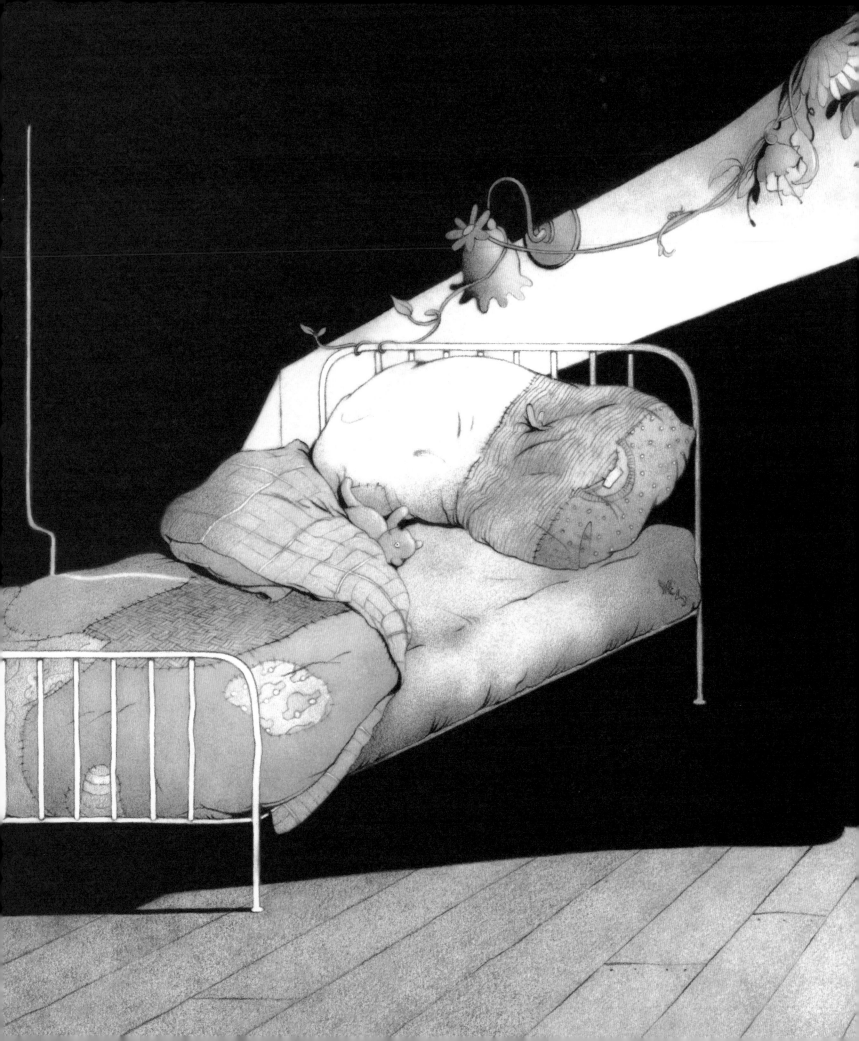

Until one morning Pandora woke
in the warmth of the sun . . .

to hear the sound of birdsong . . .

in a land of living things.

Clarion Books, 3 Park Avenue, New York, New York 10016 • Copyright © 2017 by Victoria Turnbull • All rights reserved. For information about permission
to reproduce selections from this book, write to trade.permissions@hmhco.com or to Permissions, Houghton Mifflin Harcourt Publishing Company,
3 Park Avenue, 19th Floor, New York, New York 10016. • Clarion Books is an imprint of Houghton Mifflin Harcourt Publishing Company. • www.hmhco.com
The illustrations in this book were done in colored pencil and watercolor. • The text was set in Baskerville.
Library of Congress Cataloging-in-Publication Data is available. • ISBN 978-0-544-94733-7
Manufactured in China • C&C 10 9 8 7 6 5 4 3 2 1 • 4500615264